PUFFINS OFF THE BEATEN PATH

Iceland: The Puffin Explorers Series Book 2

RA ANDERSON

Puffins Off the Beaten Path (Iceland: The Puffin Explorers Series, Book 2)

ra-anderson.com

myfavoritebookspublishingco@gmail.com

My Favorite Books Publishing Company, LLC.

Kingston, Georgia USA

Ordering Information:

Quantity sales. Special discounts are available on quantity purchases by corporations, associations, and others. Orders by U.S. trade bookstores and wholesalers. For details, contact the publisher at the address above.

Proofreading by The Pro Book Editor

Interior and Cover Design by IAPS.rocks

Photography by RuthAnne Anderson

Sketches by Hannah Jones

ISBN: 978-1-950590-08-7

Main category—JUVENILE FICTION/Science & Nature
Other category—JUVENILE FICTION/Action & Adventure

First Edition

For Cody, Cassaundra, Brody, and Zane

As evening falls on this chilly September day, a *lundi* (loon'-dee) named Árni and his best friend Birta are still missing somewhere in Iceland. Árni and Birta's parents have gathered the puffin colony together and are making a plan to find this little roaming pair! They will have to search high and low beyond this puffin cliff they call home.

Árni's father says:
Good afternoon! on this island Atlantic,
Is *Góðan daginn* in our native Icelandic!

Our son and his young puffling friend
Seem not to want their youth to end.

Árni and Birta should be off to sea,
But they are as curious as puffins can be.

It's winter's migration—time
for going, not staying,
But Árni and Birta are off somewhere playing.

A neighbor we will call upon,
Maybe he saw where they have gone.

FUN FACTS: PUFFINS COMMUNICATE!

Puffin communication takes place in the way they walk. A low-profile walk is when a puffin walks quickly with its head down. They may be saying, "Just passing through, no worries."

When guarding a burrow, a puffin may stand stiffly erect with its beak tucked in next to its body and walk with exaggerated foot movements. They may look like a soldier on guard duty, because they are. They are guarding their burrow.

Árni's father turns to a nearby
puffin and says:
Excuse me, kind puffin sir, and good day,
Have you seen Árni? He's lost his way.

The neighbor replies:
Your son and his friend took off to the south.
Young ones, always running about!
I saw them with a human kid,
Playing when they should have hid.

Mom and Dad sadly turn away,
deciding to have a look down by the bay.
The search is still on.
Where could they have gone?

FUN FACTS: PUFFIN BATTLES

As cute as puffins are, they still have to deal with other puffins. An aggressive encounter between two puffins may begin with tossing their heads and beaks up, which is called "gaping." The wider their beak is opened, the more upset the puffin is. They may even stomp their foot in place to show their displeasure. Fighting puffins bring in quite the show. Several other puffins may gather around to watch a full-scale brawl. The two fighting will lock beaks and toss one another over as if in a wrestling match.

Árni's mother says:
Farms hidden and rolling
and looking so grand
Are scattered all over our Burrow Land.

Let's fly slow to find our baby,
Hiding in the tall hay maybe?

It's true that the grass grows extra long
In a land where the sun
is up until dawn.

Iceland has cows and horses and sheep,
But they all need hay when
the snow is deep.

They produce wool, milk,
and a great treat,
Ice cream for all the people to eat.

FUN FACTS: HAY IN ICELAND

Farmers' fodder crops grow extremely well in Iceland. The long hours of daylight, cool days, and the lack of insects and pests are all beneficial to growing an abundance of hay all summer long. Iceland has less air pollution and less ground and soil pollution, which also helps the hay grow and makes it very healthy.

Árni's father says:
Look at this, dear,
Árni's human friend is here.

They cautiously approach the child,
Then see the young boy's friendly smile.

The boy scratches his head as
the two puffins stare.
How can he help? But he does seem to care.

He twists his lips, and his un-
feathered wings move.
If he had some music, he might
dance and groove.

FUN FACTS: PROTECTING PUFFINS

Puffins are not afraid of humans. Even though puffins are adorable and we would love to take them home with us, our ultimate responsibility is to protect them by not interfering with their natural habitat and way of living.

The boy flaps about, trying their fun puffin walk.
Confused by his display, the puffins wish he could talk.

And then in frustration, he stomps on the ground.
Pointing, he lets out an odd sheepish sound.

Arni's father says:
Momma, do you think? Could it possibly be?
Has this boy seen Birta and Arni?
Is he saying they went that way to help some lost sheep?
We must follow—there's no time for sleep!

Arni's mother says:
You're right! Let's go with great speed!
We must keep them safe before heading to sea!
Thank you, kind friend.
Come and see us next spring!

As the puffins fly away,
The boy waggles one featherless wing.

💡 FUN FACTS: DON'T TOUCH THE PUFFINS!

People can prevent puffin parents from performing their parental duties by simply standing around their burrows. A simple human touch can actually be very harmful for a puffin. Their feathers have a special coating that can be ruined, making them unable to survive in the cold water.

Árni and Birta are looking for twin sheep Árni found all alone in the last episode. They decided they could find and reunite them with their mother before they both have to head out to sea. It looks as if they found another four-legged friend instead.

Whoa! Árni says to the Icelandic horse.
We are exploring Iceland, of course.

Sorry our landing was such a sight.
We didn't mean to cause you a fright.

Have you seen the lost little sheep?
We must find them before they weep.

The Icelandic horse stares,
As her big nostrils flare.

The horse jerks her head, snorts, and says,
No dam would ever leave her lambs adrift!

Árni and Birta hold their heads low.
They must find the lambs before they can go.

FUN FACTS: VIKING HORSES

Icelandic Horses are descendants of the Vikings' horses brought to Iceland around the 800s (ninth century). They were shipped over from Europe's mainland by boat and needed to be small and sturdy with nice dispositions.

Árni's mother and father take flight, leaving their burrow on the cliff. They will search all of Iceland if they must, but they have to retrieve Árni and Birta before it's too late. Árni's mother sees birds, but not their little ones! She says:

With their beauty and grace,
Whooper swans are all over this place.
The only swans living in Iceland,
Whoopers must not mind the ice then.

How beautiful their long, thin necks,
Which, as they swim, they hold erect.
Through Iceland's winters some may stay,
But never in the cold, cold bay.

FUN FACTS: WHOOPER SWANS

Whooper swans fly nonstop from Scotland to Iceland during spring migration. A pilot once reported seeing a flock of whooper swans flying in a V formation at their plane's 8,000-foot cruising altitude. Scientists have recorded whooper swans flying at altitudes of up to 27,000 feet.

Instead, they winter in Iceland's northeast,
Where they can find food for a winter's feast.

Mývatn, a warm geothermal lake,
A cozy home for winter can make.

Some whooper families fly far away.
They migrate to Ireland or to the UK.

But all whooper families stick together,
Whether it's warm or cold weather.

Whoopers honk and snort and hiss,
Living together in family bliss.

Father says:
Árni and Birta are not here.
We must move along, my dear.

💡 FUN FACTS: SWAN LAKE

In Iceland, the volcanic lake Mývatn (Mee-vot) is known for bird watching, heated lagoon water, and views of the northern lights. The lake never freezes, and it attracts about 85 species of birds. Even in the winter you can find some whooper swans, but they are a migratory bird and most will spend their winters in the British Isles and Scotland areas. Whatever the reason a whooper swan may not migrate, you can find several over the winter in the Mývatn area where the lake isn't frozen and there is an ample amount of vegetation year-round.

As Árni and Birta fly on by
Another farm, Árni says. Oh my!
Let's ask this horse. He will know this farm.
Excuse me, sir, I mean no harm.

The horse says, Of course. What can I do
To help you with a question or two?

Árni says:
This farmer has no lambs, I see,
But we saw fresh fruit. How can this be?
We just saw what the farmer sold.
How can tomatoes grow in this cold?

FUN FACTS: HORSES IN WINTER

Icelandic horses are about 14.2 hands (4'9" tall) from ground to withers, and they have the ability to cope with and adjust to extreme weather conditions without being put up in barns for shelter.

The horse replies: Cucumbers, tomatoes, and even some flowers
Grow in clear barns with all-natural power.

These barns are called greenhouses, and as you've seen,
Iceland was "green" before green was keen!

They use steam and hot water from under the ground,
To make heat and energy all the year-round.

Using the Earth's non-depleting resources
Is saving our land and its creatures and horses!

Our big round Earth has considerable girth.
We should treasure all beings and all of its worth.

Árni says:
We will move on now, to further our quest,
Searching, and thank you for letting us rest.

 ## FUN FACTS: GREEN POWER!

Iceland has abundant resources of green electricity. They have hydroelectric and geothermal power plants providing water, heat, and electricity that power the artificial lighting necessary to grow crops all year at such a northerly latitude. Not all Icelanders need to purchase their utility supplies from the geothermal power plants because most have these resources in their own back yards.

Árni's mother and father fly over the swans and see several farms. They decide to stop and ask a four-legged friend about seeing the missing pufflings. Father says:

O Icelandic horses, nibbling grass,
Have you seen our son and his lass?

If you would be so kind as to please point the way,
Then you may get back to eating your hay.

If we come back someday, would
you give us a ride?
We hear that your kind have a most unique stride.

It's smooth and it's fast, if it's true what we hear,
But we must carry on now and get out of here.

You noble descendants of pure Viking horses,
Are one of this nation's most cherished resources!

FUN FACTS: GAIT HOW HORSES MOVE

Icelandic horses have an additional, unique fifth gait. This four-beat, rhythmic gait is smoother than a trot. When going slow, it is referred to as the *tölt* (turr-tl-t), but it can accelerate quickly to a much faster speed called the *skeið* (skyay-th).

Iceland is a beautiful land, but for a wandering puffin, there may be some hidden dangers lurking nearby.

Árni says:
Birta, it's an Arctic fox!
Quick, let's hide behind these rocks.

They were the only mammals here
For longer than twelve hundred years.

The fox has fearless hunting skills.
Oh, Arctic fox, you give us chills.

It's true, we struggle to take flight,
But we must soon get out of sight!

FUN FACTS: ARCTIC FOX

The Arctic fox was the first land mammal in Iceland. The Arctic fox was stranded 10,000 years ago at the end of the Ice Age, when ice broke free, disconnecting the other land formations.

When the Arctic fox looks away,
The puffins stumble, hop, and sway.

Wings fiercely flapping,
No time for napping!

They surely look like prey to him.
They gather speed, but it looks grim.

Arni says:
Sorry, fox, but we can't stay.
We've got to go far, far away!

FUN FACTS: ARCTIC FOX FUR

The white Arctic foxes' coats change from snow-white to brown in the summer to help them blend with their habitat. The blue foxes don't change colors, but the sun bleaches their fur over the summer, helping them camouflage themselves in the winter.

Árni's parents have noticed something
that's not quite right.

Oh, my dear! Momma squeaks.
Why is this family in the
middle of the street?

I'll ask them, my love, Daddy replies,
While you keep watch, it might be wise.

Halló, horned Icelandic dam,
If you will excuse me, ma'am.

What are you doing in the
middle of the road?
Árni's father asks as a lone car slows...

FUN FACTS: THE UNCHANGING ICELANDIC SHEEP

Icelandic sheep are the same genetically as they were
about 1100 years ago. They are one of Earth's oldest,
purest breeds of domestic sheep. They were brought over
with Iceland's first settlers, making it possible for people
to survive in the harsh, cold conditions.

The car stops and they hear the horned dam say,
They know we have the right of way.
Icelandic laws are on our side,
We can stop here and stand with pride.

We are a triple-purpose sheep,
From that our shepherds income reap.
Icelandic sheep are the same today,
As we've been for a thousand years, they say.

We are free to roam in the summertime,
We graze on grass and Icelandic thyme.
September comes and the gathering of sheep begins,
Rounding us up into our safe winter pens.

Árni's mother says:
We, too, are rounding up little ones.
One of them is our puffling son.

FUN FACTS: ICELAND'S SHEEP RULE THE ROAD!

These are a triple-purpose sheep—meaning they are raised for three things, like: milk, ice cream, and wool—and this is why they are well protected by law in Iceland. They are out free, grazing the land, from after they give birth to their new baby lambs in May until September.

Árni and Birta have noticed a huge burrow!
Who's burrow, is what they want to know.

Árni ponders, What could this be?
Is this a Hobbit house I see?

The cold can be so very crude,
Turf offers warmth in this latitude.

An authentic, Icelandic, green turf roof,
Could possibly warm a little sheep's hoof.

On a long winter's day,
They can snuggle in hay.

Maybe the lambs have hidden inside?
No, these doors are locked, but at least we tried.

FUN FACTS: TURF HOUSES

Turf houses were the original "green" buildings.

Each structure was built by digging into the ground, protecting it from the elements even more. The wall layers were turf from the wetlands, then they added a layer of lava stone shaped in squares, flattened the edges, and added turf again. This process would be repeated until the walls were as tall as needed.

The last turf houses were built in the 1970s. Only a few turf houses remain.

FUN FACTS: LAMBS AND DAMS

Icelandic sheep are fast and sturdy. However, they have little flocking instinct, so they roam and spread out across the land, including steep cliffs. Ewes have excellent mothering instincts. They bond quickly with their lambs and have plenty of milk to feed them. Lambs grow extremely fast, sometimes gaining twenty pounds a week.

Árni's mother says:
Let's just keep looking. We must find a clue.
I am worried, and not sure of what we should do.

A sound down below—what is that I hear?
I can't help but worry. I'm a parent, my dear.

Dear, look! Two little lambs, all alone.
They couldn't be more than two months grown.

What is the matter, my sweet little lambs?
Momma asks, as she looks all around for the dams.

Two little puffins are venturing about,
Might you have seen them while you were out?

One little lamb says, Árni left in a hurry,
But I am trying not to worry.

I don't think he noticed us, brother lamb sighs.
Let's look for our momma, his twin sister cries.

Árni's mother replies:
There's no need for you to roam,
We will help you get home!

The puffin parents lead the way, back to the road
where they'd just seen the dams. Árni's mother says:

Little Icelandic lambs, sister and brother,
We've brought you back home—here is your mother.

The mother sheep thanks them and makes sure to say,
They normally don't wander so far away.
Then she asks the puffins if they'd like to stay.
Is there anything I can help *you* with today?

Árni's father replies:
Your fleece is so lovely, so warm and so dry,
If we had more time, we might give it a try.

FUN FACTS: GATHERING SHEEP FOR WINTER

In September, farmers start to gather their sheep, a process called *Réttir* (corral) that can take up to a week. All sheep will stay on their own farms from September to May, or at least until after they give birth to their new baby lambs.

Sheep can be found anywhere in Iceland except on the glaciers, so this may take farmers, sheepdogs, people with horses, and weeks to complete. The sheep are identified by ear tags or markings, thus making it easier to know which sheep belongs with which farm.

The momma sheep says:
Some say our fleece is a pure white, you know,
But it's only *that* white with a blanket of snow.

Fiber for wool—and maybe a nest,
To keep your friends warm, yes, that would be best.

The two puffins say, We will keep this in mind,
And thank you, dear sheep, for being so kind.

But now we must find our own wandering child,
Who is having adventures out there in the wild.

The puffins wave as they take flight,
Returning to their search before it's night.

FUN FACTS: FLEECE, OR WOOL

Lopi (law'-pee) is a mix of the *tog* and *thel* fibers. It's good for making socks.

Tog (tawh) is the coarser, longer, outer fleece that is mainly used for weaving.

Thel (theth) is the softer, thicker fleece near the body of the sheep. These soft fibers are used for undergarments and baby clothes.

Fleece natural colors range from white, ivory, brown, taupe, silver, blue-gray, charcoal gray, and black. No dyes are needed, but the white fleece will hold dye well.

The two puffin parents continue their search...

They see a dark door like a tall, upright furrow.
Maybe they thought that this was a lamb's burrow.

Árni's mother says:
One thousand years ago, Icelandic man
Built turf-covered houses to live on the land.
Whether poor or rich, all were built the same.
Using turf and stone, from the earth it came.

Look at this, my love, all the structures
Were built like our burrows in nice cozy clusters.
With shared walls and mostly
tucked under the ground,
They also passed houses one generation down.
Lasting thirty to forty years, or so,
They keep whole families warm, even in snow.

FUN FACTS: HOUSES FOR FAMILY LIFE

Turf buildings in Iceland date back more than one thousand years.

The first settlers of Iceland, around 870 AD, were able to build these using materials such as turf from the wetlands, lava stone, and an extremely limited supply of wood.

These structures were built in clusters, sharing warmth and walls. They were connected with a small passageway. The main living quarters housed all of the people, with beds lining the outside walls, tables in the middle. It was where they gave birth, conceived children, and died, everything in one room.

Árni's father says:
Could you imagine a burrow this size?
It would be like living in a high-rise.
All our sisters and brothers, from Iceland to France
Could fit under this roof, he says with a glance.

From Norway and Newfoundland, Momma exclaims,
From the San Juan Islands and the coast of Maine.

From the northern seacoasts, Daddy says,
both Atlantic and Pacific,
From the US and from Russia,
it would be terrific!

And Greenland, and Labrador,
will they all fit?
No, they won't, he says.
Now let's get on with it!

It was a silent and worrisome flight,
Hoping Árni and Birta would be home by tonight.

FUN FACTS: WHERE TO SEE PUFFINS

The best place in the world to see puffins is Iceland because many of the locations are accessible by a short walk from a car. Other locations to see puffins from May-August are Great Britain; Mikines in the Faroe Islands, Denmark; Røst, Norway; in North America, Maine's Coastal Islands National Wildlife Refuge; and Witless Bay, Newfoundland, Canada.

Árni and Birta are off track, exploring Iceland and meeting all kinds of four-legged friends. Along with these four-legged friends, they spot something glowing and shimmering.

Birta says:
Eight reindeer side by side,
Can you help our little pride?

Our young lamb friends have lost their way,
And we must find them yet today.

You've roamed here since 1779.
Could you please spare us a bit of your time?

Honk or grunt to tell us the way,
Before you head for Santa's sleigh.

Birta, I think that one pointed this way
With his antler, says Árni. Thanks, reindeer! Good day!

Six thousand reindeer roaming free,
Between the farmlands and the sea.
A particle—faery dust?—starts to gleam
On one reindeer's antler. Is this a dream?

FUN FACTS: WILD REINDEER

In the 1770s, reindeer were brought over to Iceland from Norway. Farmers didn't want to farm reindeer, so they released them into the wild. There are approximately 6,000 to 7,000 reindeer living in southeastern and eastern Iceland. They blend into the landscape so well that people often don't see them grazing off the side of the main road.

A faery has spotted little Árni and Birta while the puffin parents struggle, hoping these two little one's are safe. As Mom and Dad continue to search all over Iceland, Árni's mom says:

Pufflings fledge for the sea all alone, when it's night
With no word to their parents—poof! Out of sight!

But our son is still here, and we can't find out why.
Where is he? We don't even know where to try.

Dear, we will search more after a meal.
Exploring our Iceland has been truly unreal.

We must trust that our son and his friend are okay.
Now let's look in the south, dear. What do you say?

FUN FACTS: GROWING UP

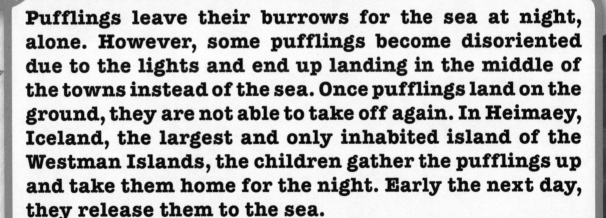

Pufflings leave their burrows for the sea at night, alone. However, some pufflings become disoriented due to the lights and end up landing in the middle of the towns instead of the sea. Once pufflings land on the ground, they are not able to take off again. In Heimaey, Iceland, the largest and only inhabited island of the Westman Islands, the children gather the pufflings up and take them home for the night. Early the next day, they release them to the sea.

The pufflings behold a magnificent sight,
unknowingly led by a mischievous sprite.

Árni and Birta find something peculiar,
An object so cool it can't be any cooler.

This ancient ice, floating, so blue and so pure,
Will start these two wanderers
on yet another detour.

From searching this island for their wooly friends,
To exploring it all till the story ends.

Forgetting the time as if they were grown,
Best friends exploring the icy unknown.

FUN FACTS: BUGS!

Author's favorite: Maybe it's because of this ancient ice, but MOSQUITOES don't exist in Iceland!

As these two little pufflings wander about, they go left when needing to go right. They stop and notice the grass has turned black, white, and blue. What is this place? They don't know! Perched upon these shapes and forms, Árni says:

FUN FACTS: THE HIDDEN PEOPLE

Many tales of trolls and elves are told in Iceland. There are still people in Iceland who truly believe in *Huldufólk* (Heul'-du-volk), the hidden people who live within the beautiful landscapes and wreak havoc on those who disturb their homes and communities.

It seems that we've left the gentle farmland,
And slipped up on something—something so grand.

The sky is still light, so we still have all day.
Maybe we'll find the lambs if we look over this way.

What's under my feet? Birta asks as she wiggles.
Árni slides on his tail. Birta slips, and she giggles.

Birta replies, Let's find someone to ask,
Someone to help with our very special task.

The little sprite gleams as she hears what they said,
The faery giggles and shakes her head.
Without a word, without a sound,
The faery waves and twinkles around.

Brewed with a wave of an arm, a storm
Of adventurous ideas starting to form,
Taking the pufflings to further explore,
This magical land from its tip to its core.

Would you like to know what these friends have found?
For fire and ice are both part of this ground.
Go grab your jacket and wear your warm socks.
We're about to explore some incredible rocks!

While the parents continue to search and explore,
Árni and Birta are learning even more.

Will you follow along as they travel this road,
Back in time to a volcanic rock episode?
To find out about Vikings and an ancient freeze,
And folkloric beings, and an earthly sneeze,
And a beach where the diamonds are loose on the sand,
And waterfalls thunder all over the land?

Days become darker with each passing hour,
As September arrives with its magical power.
In fire and ice, near the end of the day,
Adventure awaits as Árni and Birta continue to play...

PUFFINS 101: THE BASICS

The Icelandic word for puffin is *lundi*. A puffin egg incubation period is 39 to 45 days. Once hatched, the puffling's feathers are gray, resembling a little gray fluffball with a large, dark-gray beak. After 45 days of their parents' love and attention, the puffling leaves the burrow in the dark of night and heads straight to sea.

Their journey consists of bouncing and flapping their way down steep, rocky cliffs until they are safely swimming in the ocean. This is all done at night, keeping them as safe as possible from predators like the great black-backed gull.

Puffins can swim much better than they fly, so they make their way out to sea for the next three to four years. Then they typically return to the same area where they were hatched to start their own families. Puffins mate for life.

They lay one egg per year if food is plentiful. Puffins can eat small, soft fish like sand eels and herring; however, pufflings can only digest sand lance (a small, narrow fish, also called a sand eel). When these fish are scarce, puffins don't reproduce. Due to the lower numbers of sand lance, several thousands of puffins have died in the past decade.

The scarcity of sand lance is caused by several factors, including climate change (also known as global warming), oil spills, and overfishing. Creatures small and large around the world are affected by climate change. Puffins are simply one of thousands of other animal victims.

Photographer's Note: In real life, a puffling doesn't leave its burrow until the night it makes its journey to sea—this is why Árni and Birta are not little gray puffballs in my books. Instead, I have used photographs of adorable adult puffins for our dear friends Árni and Birta.

—RA Anderson, author and photographer

THE ICELANDIC LANGUAGE

The Icelandic language, *íslenska*, is well preserved, and Icelanders, *íslendingar*, are very proud of this fact. A Bible written in the 1500s can still be read by Icelanders today.

To me, most Icelandic words look like my cat walked over my keyboard, lay down, and continued mashing the keys until she heard someone opening a can of tuna and ran off.

An example of my theory is the word

Vaðlaheiðarvegavinnuverkfærageymsluskúraútidyralyklakippuhringur,

which is the longest word in the Icelandic language that I know of. Please don't ask me to pronounce it. This word means, "key ring of the key chain of the outer door to the storage tool shed of the road workers on the Vaðlaheiði." Amazing, isn't it?

I don't speak Icelandic, *íslenska*, not even the basics, but Iceland is a stunning country with impressive history and awesome people and I wanted to introduce my readers to some basic Icelandic words.

Maybe one day you will travel to Iceland to be amazed like I am about everything Iceland! Have fun learning new words!

—RA Anderson, author and photographer

GLOSSARY

aggressive: when a person or animal is behaving forcefully toward another, as if ready to argue or fight

alliance: a partnership, joining, or connection

Arctic skua: seabird that nests and breeds in Iceland, known for stealing fish from puffins and other seabirds for its food

Árni (Owrrt'-nee)

burrow: a hole in the ground that an animal like a rabbit or a puffin makes for its home

Birta (Bihrr'-tah)

Celsius (also called Centigrade)**:** scale for measuring temperature, used by most of the countries in the world except the United States and a few others.

Clowns of the Sea: nickname given to Atlantic puffins, probably because of their vivid coloring and their amusing waddle and clumsiness on land

colony: a group of one kind of animals—such as puffins—living together in one place

crevasse (also crevice)**:** deep crack or fissure in the earth or a glacier that creates a deep, narrow hole that is very dangerous to fall into

crystalize: to form or to cause something to form crystals

dam: the mother of a domestic animal, such as a mother sheep

ecosystem: a community of organisms and their environment that function as an ecological unit

environmental: the things around us that determine the area's form and character and the survival of all natural things, animals, and beings in it

equator: an imaginary line around the planet Earth that is equally distant from the north pole and the south pole and divides the planet into its northern and southern hemispheres

eruption: when a volcano, or a geyser, erupts, whatever it had been holding, like lava or boiling water, bursts suddenly out from where it had been previously hidden beneath the surface

Europe: continent on the other side of the Atlantic Ocean, also bordered by the Arctic Ocean, Asia, Africa, and the Mediterranean Sea and Black Sea

ewe: a female sheep, especially when mature

Fahrenheit: scale for measuring temperature, used mostly in the United States and a few other, smaller countries

faðir (fah-thirhh)**:** Icelandic for "father"

fjord (fyord)**:** narrow and elongated sea inlet with steep land, or cliffs, on three sides, also known as gateways

fledge: to develop the feathers necessary for a young bird to fly, and to fly away and leave the nest after growing these feathers

fleece: the coat of wool that covers a wool-bearing animal, like a sheep

flocking instinct: Most sheep have a strong flocking instinct—they are more comfortable staying together in groups and following each other around. Icelandic sheep are more independent. They have less flocking instinct and tend to wander off by themselves, with the lambs staying near their dams (mothers).

fluorescent: brightly colored, with a glowing quality

fodder: something fed to farm animals, like dried hay or feed

foreldrars: (for'-el-drars) parents

gainsay: to deny, or to claim that something is not true

gait: a specific manner of walking. Horses especially have several specific gaits, and some gaits are unique to Icelandic horses.

geothermal: relating to the heat produced and stored in the Earth's interior

geothermal [energy or power]**:** clean, renewable energy produced by the internal heat of the Earth

geothermal power plants: energy-producing facilities powered by renewable geothermal energy from the Earth

Gjáin (Djah-win)**:** an oasis in Iceland; a tiny valley with small picturesque waterfalls, tranquil ponds, and delicate volcanic structures as well as lava caves and lots of basalt columns

glaciers: large body or river of ice moving constantly but very slowly that formed near the north and south poles from hundreds of years of snow accumulating and compacting and not melting very fast. Glaciers, or ice caps, provide habitat and shelter for many native species and help regulate the atmosphere's temperature by reflecting the heat of the sun away from Earth. But the rising temperature of the oceans is melting the glaciers and endangering all that they provide to our environment.

global temperatures: average temperatures across global land and ocean surfaces. Global temperatures are measured and analyzed by NASA scientists in an ongoing study.

góðan daginn (goh-than da-yin): "Good day" in the Icelandic language

gott kvöld (gott kveld): Icelandic for "good evening"

great black-backed gull: largest of all gulls and a common predator of the puffin

green: a substance or practice that preserves the health and sustainability of the planet's environment and its inhabitants

green electricity (or green power): Electric power that comes from renewable resources and creates little or no pollution

Gullfoss (Gyeud-moss): "Golden Waterfall" in Icelandic

habitat: the place or environment where an animal or plant or person naturally, or usually, lives and grows

halló (hah-loh): "hello" in Icelandic

hand: unit of measurement traditionally used to measure a horse's height; one hand is 4 inches (10.2 centimeters)

harbinger: Something that warns of or anticipates something to come

hemisphere: the northern or southern half of the Earth when equally divided by the equator, or the eastern and western halves of the Earth when equally divided by an imaginary circle (or meridian) that passes through the north and south poles

Huldufólk (Heul-du-volk): the legendary "hidden people" of Iceland—faeries, elves, and trolls

hydroelectric (hydroelectric power): sustainable power generated from the energy of moving water

incubation period: the time between when an egg is laid and when the creature inside it hatches; Usually, the parents sit on or otherwise keep eggs warms until it's time to hatch.

inlet: recess in the shore of a body of water forming a narrow passage where water can pass through to a bay or lagoon

instinct: natural, inborn urge to do something, usually to do with the creature's own survival or the survival of its young or its family

klettur (kleh-turr): Icelandic for "cliff"

kvetch, kvetching: a Yiddish word that means to complain a lot

lagoon: a shallow seawater pond near or connected to the ocean

landscape: the physical characteristics and/or appearance of an outdoor area

latitude: imaginary lines parallel to the equator that measure distance from the equator in degrees up to ninety in either direction

lava: molten or melted rock that has been spewed out of a volcano

lopi (law'-pee): a mix of the ***tog*** and ***thel*** fibers; good for making socks

lundi (loon'-dee): "puffin" in the Icelandic language

magma: molten (melted, or liquid, because it is very hot) rock beneath the Earth's surface. When it erupts from a volcano onto the surface of the Earth, it is called lava.

migration: the act of moving from one place to another on a regular basis to be near a food supply or escape the cold, such as birds flying to warmer places each winter and then back in the spring. Birds and animals that do this are called *migratory.*

mink: an animal of the weasel family with very soft fur that was often made into winter coats, hats, and blankets to keep people warm

móðir (moh'-thirr): Icelandic for "mother"

Mývatn (Mee-vot): a warm geothermal lake in Iceland

northern lights: a natural light display seen in extreme north or south locations, near the poles

Oddny (Odd'-ny—just like it looks!)

pabbi (poppy): Icelandic for "daddy" or "papa"

peninsula: a piece of land that juts out into a body of water

population: the number of specific animals, organisms, or people who live in a certain area

predator: an animal that kills other animals for food; the animals they eat are called their *prey*

puffling: a baby puffin

ravenous: extremely hungry, devouring or gobbling food

refuge: place of shelter or protection from danger or difficulty; where something or someone can live in safety

resources: natural resources are the things in a given area that and provide residents with things they need to survive

Réttir (Rrrii-yat-tirrh): annual event in Iceland in September, when farmers gather their wandering sheep to bring them to shelter for the winter

Sandlance: (Ammodytidae fish family and sometimes called a sand eel) They are a slender silver fish with a fork tail, long dorsal fin, and a pointed nose. They are bottom dwellers found living in the sand under the surf. They are around 20 to 46 centimeters long and are found in the North seas.

Scotland: The northernmost country in the United Kingdom, Scotland is about 1200 kilometers, or about 750 miles, from Iceland. Some birds, including whooper swans, migrate between Iceland and Scotland.

Sea Parrot: nickname given to Atlantic puffins, probably because of their vivid coloring.

settler: someone or some creature that moves into a new area and decides to stay

silica: a compound of the elements silicon and oxygen that occurs naturally in sand and quartz

skeið (skyay-th): a gait of the Icelandic horse, like the *tölt* but faster

soil pollution: toxic chemicals, enough to endanger the health of people or the environment, usually from industrial activity, pesticides or insecticides, or waste that has not been properly disposed of

species: a group of organisms that share important characteristics, such as how they live, how they have babies, and how they find food. They look for mates among their own kind. Scientists group species together into larger families. The Atlantic puffin is a species that lives on the Atlantic coast. There are other puffin species on the Pacific coast, and all of them are members of a large group of seabirds called the alcid family.

stratovolcano: a volcano formed by many layers of built-up lava and ash

survive: to stay alive

thel (theth): the softer, thicker fleece near the body of the sheep; these soft fibers are used for undergarments and baby clothes

tog (tawh): the coarser, longer, outer fleece of a sheep that is mainly used for weaving

tölt (turr-tl-t): a gait of the Icelandic horse, like a very smooth trot

tourist: someone who travels to a place for the purpose of seeing its natural and historical sights or experiencing its recreation or entertainment opportunities

turf: the upper layer of earth held together by grasses; sod

twilight: the time between sunset and the full dark of night, or the light during that time

V formation: the formation that migrating birds fly in when migrating, shaped like the letter V

Vatnajökull (Vat'-na-yo-geut): Icelandic for "the river glacier" and is nicknamed "The Big One." Iceland's largest glacier.

vik (vig): a creek or inlet or small bay

Viking: In old Norse, this was **vikingr**, which means "freebooter," "sea-rover," "pirate," and "Viking." They are people who came from the fjords, or *vik* areas of Scandinavia.

weaving: to make cloth or a basket by intertwining pieces of thread, wool yarn, grasses, or thin strips of wood

webbed feet: feet with skin connecting the toes, like a sail; found mostly in animals who live part of their lives in the water, like ducks and puffins

wetlands: an area and ecosystem that is always or seasonally covered in shallow water, where lots of aquatic plants live

withers: the ridge between the shoulder bones of a horse at the highest part of a horse's back, lying at the base of the neck above the shoulders. The height of a horse is measured to the withers.

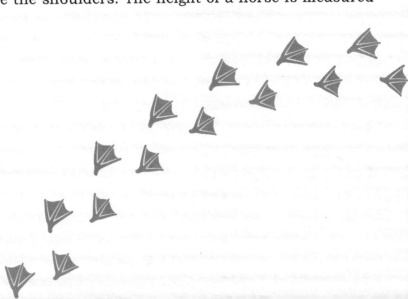

ABOUT THE AUTHOR

RA Anderson is a wanderer who has lived all over, from California to Belize, and currently, home is a town called Rome, in Georgia that is! She grew up on horseback and sailboats—"the most amazing way to grow up!"

A lifelong passion for creative writing and photography became her life. Her award-winning photographs have been featured in table books, magazines, and front-page news, and her writing has been published in magazines, poetry books, and children's books.

Three boys—her heart and soul—call her Mom. She and her husband—"my strength and passion"—are recent empty-nesters, leaving them more time to travel.

"My life is full, colorful, and exhausting, and I wouldn't trade it for anything. However, people seem to think my most impressive accomplishment is that I know how to work the manual settings on a DSLR camera!"

OTHER BOOKS BY RA ANDERSON

If Pets Could Talk: Dogs

If Pets Could Talk: A Service Dog

If Pets Could Talk: Cats

If Pets Could Talk: Farm Animals

Girl Sailing Aboard the Western Star

ACKNOWLEDGEMENTS

Iceland: The Puffin Explorers wouldn't be possible without the influence and assistance of several people.

—My gratitude to my son Cody and his wife Cassaundra for asking for my assistance with their wedding. If they had not decided to get married in Iceland, none of this would have happened.

—I am grateful for my husband's support and patience with me throughout this whole process, and for the past thirty-plus years.

—Thank you to Brody, Zane, and my parents for traveling with me to Iceland.

—To all of my family (Anderson, Lewis, Hite, Schlitz, and Simons) who cheered me on, I thank you.

—And a huge thank you to my edit team with Debra L. Hartmann, the Pro Book Editor, who has taught me so much!

CPSIA information can be obtained
at www.ICGtesting.com
Printed in the USA
LVHW072128191219
641156LV00001B/1/P